AFRICAN FOLKTALES, FABLES AND LEGENDS

A. KWADA

Copyright © 2020 A. Kwada

All rights reserved.

ISBN: 9781657147430

DEDICATION

This book is dedicated to all African cultures.

CONTENTS

ACKNOWLEDGMENTS i

1 ONIYEYE AND KING OLUDOTUN'S DAUGHTER............................1

2 MOREMI (YORUBA LEGEND FROM NIGERIA) 5

3 THE GRASSHOPPER AND THE BROKEN CALABASH
(KAMWE PEOPLE OF NORTHERN NIGERIA)......................................8

4 THE WRESTLING CONTEST BETWEEN THE CAT AND THE
TORTOISE 15

5 THE ORIGIN OF CATTLE
(FROM THE MAASAI PEOPLE OF KENYA) 19

6 THE WISE DOG 21

7 THE WOMEN'S CATTLE (FROM THE MAASAI PEOPLE OF
KENYA) 24

8 ELEPHANT AND HARE (MASSAI) 26

9 TWO BROTHERS WHO WERE FRIENDS (MAASAI) 30

10 THE GIRLS OF THE KNEE (MAASAI) 34

11 WHY PEOPLE HAVE TO DIG (LUHYA OF KENYA) 38
12 WHY ZEBRAS HAVE STRIPED SKINS (LUHYA) 42
13 KALISANGA AND KALIYETO (LUHYA) 46
14 THE TORTOISE WHO FLE (A FOLKTALE FROM ZIMBABWE)
.... 51
15 THE LEGEND OF SHAKA ZULU (SOUTH AFRICA) 56
16 THE GRASSHOPPER AND THE TOAD 58
17 THE TORTOISE AND THE PRINCESS WHO NEVER SPEAKS ... 60
18 THE THREE BROTHERS AND THE POT OF PORRIDGE 63
19 HOW THE CHIMPANZEES BOTTOM GOT SWOLLEN AND RED 66
20 THE LOST HEIR 69
21 WHY MOSQUITOES BUZZ IN PEOPLE'S EARS 73
REFERENCE 76

ACKNOWLEDGMENTS

I want to thank those who in one way or the other have contributed to the development of this book.

1 ONIYEYE AND KING OLUDOTUN'S DAUGHTER

Long ago there lived a king called Oludotun. He had only one child a very beautiful daughter. When she reached a marriageable age, her father was unable to decide on suitable husband for her. Many young men had asked for the girl as wife, but the king had refused them all. At last, in order to rid himself of the many suitors, he announced that he would give his daughter's hand in marriage, and half the kingdom, to any man who could bring him an animal with one hundred and fifty-two tails. All the hunters received this news with great surprise. Oniyeye, the best hunter of all, made up his mind that if such an animal existed in the world would hunt it down.

First, he went to an Ifa priest and asked if there was really such an animal. The priest, for a small gift, consulted his jujus. "Yes", he said, "such an animal does exist, but only one remains in the whole world. It lives in a hollow mountain far away. Nobody can reach it except in their dreams. If you like to dream of it, you must make a sacrifice to the gods on waking. I can tell you nothing more."

Oniyeye thanked the priest and went away to think. At last he had an idea. He told all his friends that he was going away on a long journey. He set out with his bow and arrows and his hunter's talisman, and travelled for several days until he reached an area where there were many wild animals. He stopped in an open glade and lay down with his quiver under his head and his bow under his, pretending to be dead.

For a long time oniyeye lay perfectly still, waiting. Then a tiny field-mouse appeared, and watched him from a distance. Oniyeye did not move. The mouse came up close and looked at his face. (He knew this was oniyeye, for all the animals knew of his great skill as a hunter, and knew him by his talisman.) The field mouse started to sing and call all other animals to come and see. One by one they came to the glade until it was full of animals rejoicing at the death of the hunter and calling their friends to spread the news. The animal with one hundred and fifty-two tails heard the news from some birds who passed the hollow mountain on their way home. He sent them back to tell the animals to prepare for his arrival. When the animal with one hundred and fifty-two tails came to the glade, all the other animals were impressed and prostrated themselves, hailing him as their king.

"This is a great day," said the animal. "I shut myself up in the hollow mountain for many years because of this great hunter. Now he is dead, I shall live among you all." The animals gave a roar of applause, and the animal with one hundred and fifty-two tails become boastful. "Pick up the dead oniyeye." he ordered, "and let me ride him like a horse."

The oniyeye sprang up, bow and arrows in hand. In their sudden fear all the animals ran away, leaving their king unprotected. The animal with one hundred and fifty-two tails begged the hunter to spare his life, and promised to be his slave.

So oniyeye led the strange animal back to the king's palace, and people came from far and wide to see it. Oniyeye married the king's daughter and ruled over half the kingdom. The animal with one hundred and fifty-two tails lived peacefully in captivity, and the other animals lived in greater security, for oniyeye did not go hunting so often after his marriage.

Adapted from Fourteen cowries

By Abayomi fuja (Ibadan Univ, press 1967)

2 MOREMI (YORUBA LEGEND FROM NIGERIA)

Long time ago, There lived a beautiful woman called Moremi Ajasoro who was a princess from Offa. She was married to Oranmiyan who is the Onni of Ile-Ife at that time. Moremi was not only a very beautiful woman, she was also brave, patriotic and loved her people. The people of Ile- Ife suffered a great deal from raids of the Igbo invaders, dressed in raffia palms, who usually attack from the forest. People of Ile-Ife were too scared to stand their ground, because the invaders looked like evil spirits of the forest, not people. And this continued in an unrelenting fashion year after year. Every time the invaders attack the people will flee shouting 'The forest devils are coming! Run for your lives! It came to a point in time in which Oranmiyan became so disturbed to the extent that he became so nervous and troubled.

Moremi decided that she had to do something in order to restore her husband's happiness and bring peace to the people of Ile-Ife. One day, she went to a stream called Esenmerin, to approach the Orisa or river goddess in order to seek for solution to the incessant problem caused by their fearsome enemies. The river goddess offered to help her but at a price to which Moremi agreed and said if the goddess is going to help her, then she is ready to pay any price.

The goddess advised Moremi that when next the Igbo raiders came, she should allow herself to be captured and being a very pretty woman, the next time they came, she allowed herself to be captured and was taken away. When the Ruler of the Igbo raiders saw her, he fell in love with her and took her as his queen. Within a short period of time she has integrated herself within the palace and the society. And the king and his people admired Moremi's wisdom and beauty, even though she was a foreigner, they came to trust her. Soon she found out that the so called "devils" who attacked Ile-Ife were simply Igbo men in disguise covered with raffia palm from head to toe, in order to become invisible while attacking Ile-Ife. She also discovered that lighted torches can destroy the Igbo marauders raffia coverings. Having discovered this secret she waited for a golden opportunity and escaped back to Ile-Ife armed with the information. When she arrived Ile-Ife she conveyed this information to the king and the elders, for which they were glad and happy and they all waited patiently for next time the Igbo invaders would come.

The next time the forest devils attacked, the people of Ile-Ife were ready for them with lighted torches. They pursued them, setting fire to their raffia coverings while they flee like fireflies into the forest. The people of Ile-Ife rejoiced.

After that the river goddess appeared to Moremi and asked for the fulfillment of the promise earlier made, to which Moremi brought a Cow as well as a Ram. But the goddess rejected these, saying that it was Moremi's son, Olurogbo that she wanted as a sacrifice. Moremi had no option than to offer her only son.

As a result of the huge loss to Moremi, the people of Ile-Ife as well as the elders promised to be her sons and daughters.

Thus from that day onwards, the Edi festival was instituted as a remembrance to the heroic deeds of this beautiful princess, who saved her people from the raiding activities of Igbo warriors. Furthermore a number of places are named after her in contemporary Nigeria such as the female resident halls at the University of Lagos and Obafemi Awolowo University. And also there is a bust of her in the centre of Ile-Ife.

3 THE GRASSHOPPER AND THE BROKEN CALABASH
(KAMWE PEOPLE OF NORTHERN NIGERIA)

Once upon a time in a land called Mwe, there lived a young farmer called Tumba and his wife kwasini. They are both very hard working and worked diligently on their guinea corn farm from day to day, as it was the rainy season and the weeds are fast growing. They lived in a small compound with three mud huts surrounded by a wall of bamboo stalks. One day as they were working on their farm, Tumba caught a grasshopper and gave it to his wife to keep but mistakenly, the grasshopper left the grip of Kwasini and flew away. Out of rage Tumba shouted "You must! Get me that grasshopper or else you must go back to your father's house!" Out of love for her husband, kwasini decided to pursue the grasshopper in order to please her husband. And she is pregnant with a child. Each time she pursued the grasshopper and tries to catch it, it always fly's off and land at a distance. Unknown to her, she was getting closer to the forbidden forest as her mind was fixed on the grasshopper. It was later that she realized her presence in the forbidden forest and it was getting dark. While trying to find her way back, she felt a sharp pain in her and at that point she knows her child wants to come out. With labour pains, she keeps on breathing heavily as she moves with some effort, till she came across a large grimy house, built with black stones. She wasn't sure it was the right thing to do but she gather up her courage and went inside because she was in pain. The inside was slightly lit by an old bush lamp where an old hag whose face was horror some sat. Kwasini wants to speak but the pain was intense and immediately the old hag got up and walked with a hunch towards kwasini and she held her. She then told her "You shouldn't be here my child but i will help you." She then helped her delivered the baby and gave her food and water. Kwasini was so glad that she didn't know how to thank this old woman even though she looks scary. The old lady then told her "you are lucky my child, you could have died." "Thank you so much," replied Kwasini "I can't pay you enough," "my child," said the old lady "This house is not a place for you, it is the house of the dead and they made me their caretaker," kwasini was now horrified "Any moment from dawn they will all be coming back from their hunt, so you must leave before that time but not now because you need to rest." Even though she was filled with fear kwasini still had a sense of relief from the warm words of the old lady. So very early before dawn the old lady showed kwasini the way out of the forest and bid her goodbye while the baby was slightly clenched in her arms, warmly.

At home, Tumba was delighted to see his wife with the new born baby and he couldn't wait but to call the village for celebration, for it was their first child. After that, Kwasini handed over to him the grasshopper to his delight, then she told him "I nearly lost my life because of that thing, if not for the old lady in the forest, I could have been dead by now." One early morning Kwasini served her husband some hot porridge in a calabash but while Tumba was about to take a sip of the porridge the calabash slipped off his hands and fell to the ground broken in half. Kwasini heard the sound and came out of the kitchen hut to see what happened. And Tumba knows from the look on her face what he got himself into. "You have to fix! My calabash for me or else I will leave your house for you!"

"My wife how can I fix this? It's broken already," Tumba asked sympathetically, "I want you to fix it by stitching it up with a hair from the mane of a young Lion or else! Hmmm.." Tumba was now troubled, he wondered how he could fulfill his loving wife's request. Therefore he set out for a journey into the forbidden forest. While On the journey, He came across the same large grimy house made with black stones and he timidly step inside because he needed a place to pass the night. To his surprise the same old scary hag welcomed him as if she knew him. She gave him food to eat and a place to sleep. She then later asked him "did you lost your way my son?"

"Not really…" he replied, "I am on a quest to find a hair from the mane of a young lion,"

"Mane of a young lion?", "Yes" he replied as he cleared his throat. He then went on and narrated the issue to the old lady, "Interesting?" she replied. "well if you haven't explained this to me, I would have cooked you in the morning for the dead,"

"For this is their house and I am their caretaker" horrified with what he heard Tumba's heart beat was now at its maximum,

"please I beg you! Don't kill me!" he sympathize out of fear,

"hmm… My son don't be afraid I will not kill but I will help you but under one condition" Tumba was now a bit delighted "I will do! Anything,"

"hmm.. You must grind four bags of millet for me with a grinding stone before midnight,"

"Ok!" he replied knowing the heavy task he was about to do. After the hard labour, she then told him to hide inside the roof of one the rooms, the dead use to keep their wild animals.

When it was dawn the dead start to arrive with howls, cries and voices that sounded like a dragon's breath. When they all settled, they started complaining "what's that nice smell!",
"it smells like fresh blood!"
"No it smells like human flesh!" The old lady was serving them food but their noses were high in the air not caring about what was placed before them. The old lady then said "Stop fooling yourselves, there is nothing here!"
"You sure?" they asked "Yes very sure, now eat! Your food, you morons!" When they are done with their food, they immediately retire to their rooms to sleep and placed their wild animals in their rooms too. After a long time of silence, Tumba then heard a whisper "You can now come down and get your hair," Tumba silently came down and located a young lion sleeping close by, and he cautiously removed a single strand of hair from its mane and left silently. The old hag told him to leave quickly and never to stop.

When the dead awoke at twilight they began to prepare to set out. As usual they began the normal counting of the hairs of their animals, for they are precious to them. But to their surprise, one hair was missing from one of the young Lions.
"I counted it! Before I slept but now one is missing! How impossible!"

"Are you sure!" shouted one of them "I have three hundred eyes! How can i not be sure!"

"Then a thief must have stolen it!",

"we must get him!",

"He will come to us!" Then the dead began singing the song

"Back! Back! Back! ...back! Back! Back!!

Whoever stole from the dead move!

Back! Back! Back! ...back! Back! Back!!

Whoever stole the hair of our lion move!

Back! Back! Back! ...back! Back! Back!!

He shall be our meal today! Move!

Back! Back! Back! ...back! Back! Back!! "

While Tumba was walking he noticed something unusual, instead of moving forward, he began to move backward. Then the old lady shouted "stop!" Then there was silence as the dead all turned to listen to their caretaker, "Have you morons! Forgotten that you are supposed to say 'forward' instead of 'back'? "

"Use forward not 'back!' " then they all started singing "Forward! Forward! Forward! ....." Tumba then noticed himself moving forward, quickly and not backward till he was out of the forbidden forest. Now with the hair, he stitched his wife's calabash and gave it to her and up till now the dead are still singing their song but no one came and they keep singing and singing and singing……

4 THE WRESTLING CONTEST BETWEEN THE CAT AND THE TORTOISE

In the country of the animals, the Cat was regarded as the champion wrestler of the animals , for he had so far managed to throw everybody who had challenged him. It was, therefore, not surprising that he enjoyed great popularity, and his friendship was eagerly sought after. One day the tortoise came to call on the cat and invited him to visit and accept his hospitality. Now the Cat had been warned that the tortoise was a very clever and deceitful person, so when the Tortoise invited him to his home, he did not want to go. He made excuses and put off the visit.

The tortoise was far from snubbed by the Cat's refusal, and continued to press his unwanted friendship. At last the cat, more for the sake of peace and quiet than for friendship's sake, agreed to visit the Tortoise. When he arrived he was surprised, for the

Tortoise had prepared a large and very fine fish and plenty of palm wine, fufu and kola nuts. Now the Cat was very fond of all these things and he sat down beside his host and enjoyed the feast. Having eaten to his satisfaction, he lay down and stretched himself out under the cool shade of some large banana leaves, thinking sleepily to himself that the Tortoise was not such a bad fellow after, and that the reports about him had been incorrect.

After this the two animals became close friends and were often to be seen seated under the shade of the banana leaves in the Tortoise's compound. One day, some little time after this, the Tortoise suddenly asked the Cat how he managed to become a champion wrestler and throw animals that appeared to be so much stronger than himself. "Ah," said the Cat, "you see I have a powerful juju which I use when I wrestle; in this way I am able to throw all comers. It is very indeed."

"Tell me, my friend," said the Tortoise, "how many jujus you have, and what they are. Perhaps I am asking for too much information, but I am very interested in your great powers, and I am your friend."

"That is very easy," answered the Cat, "I am willing to tell you, I have two jujus that I use," and the Cat related what they were. Now the Cat was very clever and not such a fool as the Tortoise imagined, for in actual fact he used three jujus for his wrestling contests. He did not tell the Tortoise about the third one. Sometime later, all the animals were very surprised indeed to learn that the Tortoise had taken up wrestling. At first they laughed a lot at the idea of a Tortoise wrestling, but as the Tortoise continued to win contest after contest against all comers, their surprise and admiration grew. Meanwhile, the Cat watched with great amusement, but said nothing. As the Tortoise defeated each comer, his conceit grew, until the day came that the Cat had been waiting for.

"Why don't you challenge the Cat?" said all the tortoise's supporters. "You are now the strongest animal amongst us, and the Cat has been successful for ages and we have noticed that he has not challenged anybody for long time. Now is your chance to become the champion wrestler in the land of the animals. Try throwing the Cat."

"Yes." replied the conceited animal, "now I will throw the Cat and make him acknowledge me as the champion wrestler in the land. Go and arrange a day for the contest."

On the day appointed, there was a greater gathering of animals with much excitement and talk on the merit and chances of both contestants. An open space was marked off and the animals sat down outside to watch what promised to be the most interesting wrestling match ever held, for neither side had ever been defeated. In the first bout both the Cat and the Tortoise used the first juju, and after a great struggle a draw was announced.

In the second bout the animals used the second juju, and another great tussle' ensued, without either animal overcoming the other. This too declared a draw. The tortoise now suggested that they should share the championship between them, but all the animals called out for third and final round to settle the matter.

Having no more jujus, the Tortoise decided to use a combination of the first and second juju. The Cat, of course, used his third juju, with the result that the Tortoise was soundly beaten. And ever afterwards the Tortoise has taken good care to avoid both the Cat and the wrestling ring. If you have a friend do not try to fight him even if you think you know his secrets

(Adapted from Fourteen Hundred Cowries by Abayomi Fuje9(I.U.P), 1967)

5 THE ORIGIN OF CATTLE
(FROM THE MAASAI PEOPLE OF KENYA)

In the beginning, the Maasai did not have any cattle. One day God called Maasinta, who was the first Maasai and said to him: "I want you to make a large enclosure, and when you have done so, come back and inform me." Maasinta went and did as he was instructed, and came back to report what he had done. Next God said to him: "Tomorrow, very early in the morning, I want you to go and stand against the outside wall of the house for I will give you something called cattle. But when you see or hear anything do not be surprised. Keep very silent."

Very early in the morning, Maasinta went to wait for what was to be given him. He soon heard the sound of thunder and God released a long leather thong from heaven to earth. Cattle descended down this thong into the enclosure. The surface of the earth shook so vigorously that his house almost fell over. Maasinta was gripped with fear, but did not make any move or sound. While the cattle were still descending, the Dorobo, who was a housemate of Maasinta, woke up from his sleep. He went outside and on seeing the countless cattle coming down the strap, he was so surprised that he said: "Ayieyieyie!" and exclamation of utter shock. On hearing this, God took back the thong and the cattle stopped descending. God then said to Maasinta, thinking he was the one who had spoken: "Is it that these cattle are enough for you? I will never again do this to you, so you had better love these cattle in the same way I love you." That is why the Maasai love cattle very much. How about the Dorobo? Maasinta was very upset with him for having cut God's thong. He cursed him thus: "Dorobo, are you the one who cut God's thong? May you remain as poor as you have always been. You and your offspring will forever remain my servants. Let it be that you will live off animals in the wild. May the milk of my cattle be poison if you ever taste it." This is why up to this day the Dorobo still live in the forest and they are never given milk.

6 THE WISE DOG

A Strange thing occurred in the country of animals. There came a period of great strife and trouble, with many bitter fights and much hardship. Everything seemed to go wrong. It was as if a great curse had descended on all of them.

The king of animals called a great meeting. Something must be done to put things right. All the animals agreed on this point, but what were they to do, what was the cause of their misfortune? They argued over the matter for a very long time. Many suggestions were put forward, but no conclusions were reached. Then somebody suggested that all their troubles could be traced back to the days of their early youth, and if anybody was to be blamed it must be their mothers. Yes, their mothers were to blame for the whole thing. Had they not been responsible for bringing them up? Had they not allowed them to play about when they should have been doing other things? Were their mothers not always interfering with them in the days of their youth? They had been handicap all through. So the animals looking for a scapegoat on which to pin their subsequent misfortunes found one ready to hand in their mothers. The idea spread like bush fire in the dry season. "We must kill all our mothers to punish them for our misfortunes and appease the gods," they all screamed. Every animal was to kill his own mother.

There was only one animal who was not carried away with this evil idea. He was the dog, who greatly respected his mother. He was too wise an animal to be carried away by their foolish words, but he had sufficient intelligence to see that it was hopeless to go against the wishes of all the other animals. So the dog quietly acquiesced to the idea of everybody killing their own mothers. The great slaughter of mothers commenced. The dog, fearing that, if he hid his mother, the other animals would discover her hiding place and slaughter them both, sent her to heaven.

The dog's mother was very grateful for her son's kindness and consideration. When she was about to depart, she told him that if ever he was in any trouble or want, he had only to call on her and she would help him. She then taught him a little song when in trouble. The animals were soon to know that the killing of their mothers had not helped matters very much; for the next season brought a terrible famine to the land. The water holes dried up, there was no meat, all the crops failed, and many animals died. The dog, remembering his mother's parting words, went out to a quiet and unfrequented part of the bush and sang:

O, Mother, O Mother, send down your cord.

Take your son up to heaven and feed him today;

For he needs your help now and remembers your words.

O, please Mother, O Mother, O Mother.

Immediately, a cord descended from heaven and at the end of it hung a tiny bench. The dog sat himself on the little bench and was pulled up through the clouds to heaven. When he reached heaven, his mother feasted him and did everything she could to make him happy, and when evening came he was let down again into the starving country of animals. Each day while the famine lasted, the dog would go and sing his song, and the cord would descend and take him up to visit his mother in heaven.

  Adapted from Fourteen cowries

7 THE WOMEN'S CATTLE
(FROM THE MAASAI PEOPLE OF KENYA)

One morning before the cattle were taken out to graze, a cow was slaughtered. Soon the cattle started moving away to graze by themselves and wandered off. One woman told another woman's child to go and drive the cattle back before they went too far. When the child's mother heard this she said: "Oh no, my child is not going until he has eaten the kidney." It followed that whenever a child was asked to go, his mother forbade him to go until he had a bite of the meat. This went on until all the cattle, sheep and goats wandered away into the bush and got lost. When all the children had eaten the meat, they tried to bring the cattle back, but they found that they had all gone wild. And so that is how it came about that women lost their cattle. They then went and lived with the men who had all along taken good care of their cattle. This is why up to this very day, all the cattle belong to the men and women simply wait for the men to provide for them.

8 ELEPHANT AND HARE (MASSAI)

There was once a herd of elephants who went to gather honey to take to their in-laws. As they were walking along, they came upon Hare who was just about to cross the river. She said to one of them: "Father, please help me get across the river." The elephant agreed to this request and said to Hare: "You may jump on to my back." As Hare sat on the elephant's back, she was quick to notice the two bags full of honey that the elephant was carrying. She started eating honey from one of the bags, and when she had eaten it all, she called out to Elephant saying: "Father, please hand me a stone to play with." When she was given the stone, she put it in the now empty bag of honey, and started eating the honey from the second bag. When she had eaten it all, she again requested another stone saying: "Father, please hand me another stone for the one you gave me has dropped, and I want to throw it at the birds." Elephant handed her another stone, and then another, as she kept asking for stones on the pretext that she was throwing them at the birds, until she had filled both bags with stones. When Hare realised that the elephants were about to arrive at their destination, she said to the elephant which was carrying her: "Father, I have now arrived, please let me down." So Hare went on her way. Soon afterwards, the elephant looked at his bags, only to realise that they were full of stones! He exclaimed to the others: "Oh my goodness! The hare has finished all my honey!" They lifted up their eyes and saw Hare leaping away at a distance; they set off after her. They caught up with Hare within no time, but as the elephants were about to grab her, she disappeared into a hole. But the elephant managed to catch hold of her tail, at which time the skin from the tail got peeled off. Elephant next grabbed her by the leg. Hare laughed at this loudly, saying: "Oh! You have held a root mistaking it for me!" Thereupon Elephant let go of Hare's leg and instead got hold of a root. Hare shrieked from within and said: "Oh father, you have broken my leg!" As Elephant was struggling with the root, Hare maneuvered her way out and ran as fast as her legs could carry her. Elephant had by this time managed to pull out the root only to realise that it was not Hare's leg. Once more he lifted up his eyes and saw Hare leaping and jumping over bushes in a bid to escape. Elephant ran in pursuit of her once more. As Hare continued running, she came across some herdsmen and said to them: "Hey you, herdsmen, do you see that elephant from yonder, you had better run away, for he is coming after you." The herdsmen scampered and went their separate ways. When Elephant saw the herdsmen running, he thought they were running after Hare; so he too ran after them. When he caught up with them, he said: "Hey you, herdsmen, have you seen a hare with a skinned tail passing along here?" The herdsmen answered: "You have passed her along the way as she was going in the opposite direction." While Elephant had been chasing the herdsmen, Hare had gained some time to run in the opposite direction.

Next, Hare came upon some women who were sewing outside the homestead and said to them: "Hey you, mothers who are sewing, do you see that elephant from yonder, you had better run away for he is coming after you." On hearing this, the women scampered for the safety of their houses immediately. But soon the elephant caught up with them and asked: "Hey you, honourable ladies, might you have seen a hare with a skinned tail going toward this direction?" The women answered: "There she goes over there."

Hare kept running and this time she came upon antelopes grazing and she said to them: "Hey you, antelopes, you had better run away for that elephant is coming after you." The antelopes were startled and they ran away as fast as their legs could carry them. But soon the elephant was upon them, and he asked them: "Hey you, antelopes, have you seen a hare with a skinned tail going in this direction?" They pointed out to him the direction that Hare had followed.

Still on the run, Hare next came upon a group of other hares, to whom she said: "Hey you, hares, do you see that elephant coming from yonder? You should all skin your tails for he is after those hares with unskinned tails." Thereupon all the hares quickly skinned their tails. At the same moment the elephant arrived and asked them: "Hey you, hares, have you seen a hare with a skinned tail going towards this direction?" The hares replied: "Don't you see that all our tails are skinned?" As the hares said this, they were displaying their tails confident it would please Elephant. On noticing that all the hares' tails were skinned, Elephant realised that Hare had played a trick on him. Elephant could not find the culprit, for all the hares were alike. And there ends the story.

9 TWO BROTHERS WHO WERE FRIENDS (MAASAI)

There once lived two step-brothers who were such close friends that no one could separate them. One of the boys lost his mother at an early age, so the surviving wife was charged with the responsibility of taking care of both boys. And this woman, who was the boy's step-mother, had no liking for her step-son. And the boy's duty was to look after cattle, among which was one gentle cow that the boys used to milk each day whenever they became hungry. Each of the boys drew from two of the cow's four teats, and this became a rule which they always observed. The boys referred to each other as "son of my father" because they were the sons of one man. Their mother, as the surviving wife came to be called by both boys, did not like the idea of the two boys being such good friends, and so tried unsuccessfully to separate them. She said to herself, "I must find a way of killing this boy." So, the next day, as the boys took the cattle out grazing, she told her own son to return home at the middle of the day to have a haircut. The boy did as he was bid, and at around midday he went back home, had a haircut and a drink of milk and returned to the cattle. The next day it was the turn of the other boy to have his hair cut. But before the boy went home, the woman dug a deep hole at the head of the bed. On arrival the boy was sent to fetch a razor from the head of the bed. But as he tried to rummage for the blade he fell into the hole, which the woman quickly covered with a big stone. The other boy waited expectantly for his friend until the evening when he drove the cattle back home, assuming that his friend must have been assigned some other duty at home.

As soon as he got home the boy looked for his step-brother; but not finding him he asked his mother where he was. She categorically denied having any knowledge of his whereabouts, saying: "I gave him a haircut and he went back to the cattle." The people looked for the boy everywhere, and when they could not find him, they assumed he had been eaten by wild animals. After some time, the villagers moved home and burnt up the old village. When the rains fell, some long grass grew at the old settlement. One day the surviving boy, who had cried for his brother until he could cry no more, took the cattle there to graze. While the cattle grazed he went and sat down on the big stone that covered the hole inside which was his brother. It so happened that the boys had a song they used to sing when they were milking their cow; and, as he sat on the stone, the boy remembered his step-brother and started singing the song:

Son of my father

The udder of the dapple grey is bursting with milk

But I will not draw from your teats

Son of my father.

When the boy in the hole heard the other one singing he responded in song:

Son of my father

You may draw and let it nurture you

Son of my father

It was your mother who put me into the hole.

 When the boy on the top of the stone first heard the reply he thought his voice was simply being echoed by the forest. He sang one more time, and again his brother sang in response, so he realised that the singing was coming from underneath the stone.

On rolling the stone away he was astonished to see his brother, whom he helped out of the hole. He had eaten soil and his clothes were all tattered. He could barely see, for his eyes had grown sensitive to light. The boy gave his brother clothes to put on, and he milked one of the cows for him to drink fresh milk. He first made him vomit all the soil he had been eating, and then fed him with some fresh milk. When evening came, he took him home with him. On their way home the boy who had been rescued related to his step-brother how their mother had put him inside the hole. His step-brother became furious because he loved his brother more than any other person. When they were about to reach home, he sharpened his spear till it was razor sharp. On arrival he headed straight for his mother, whom he instantly speared to death. He next sought his father to inform him of what he had done. The men were then assembled, and when the story was told the people simply listened without comment. Nothing could be done. So the boys lived happily without a mother.

10 THE GIRLS OF THE KNEE (MAASAI)

Once upon a time, there lived a cruel old man. His wife conceived; but, as was his habit, the old man did not like seeing her take a rest. As soon as she had completed one task, she was told to take on another. And no sooner had she completed the second task, than she was commanded to take up yet another. This routine was repeated every day, from morning till night, so that the poor old woman, though pregnant, was kept on her feet each day until the early hours of the morning. And so, many months went by. The woman persevered and kept on working, since her husband would never permit her to rest. She would wake up every morning before dawn to do the milking, after which she would lock up the calves in their pens. Having done this she would scamper to the river to fetch water for the household. Then firewood. It was also her duty to plaster the house. Every single job around the home was supposed to be her responsibility. And as though that was not enough, she was often called upon to water the cattle while her husband rested at home. The old man kept pestering his wife thus until one day, overwhelmed with fatigue, she collapsed and died. She was seven months pregnant.

 The morning after his wife died the old man woke up with a large swelling on one knee. At first he thought it was a boil, but the swelling grew bigger and heavier by the day, until the old man could barely walk. After what seemed like months the old man's patience wore out. He took a knife and said to himself: "Since this boil is never coming to a head, I am going to lance it come what may." And as he lanced the boil, to his great surprise, there emerged two adorable little girls. Amazed as he was at this strange occurrence, the old man was nevertheless delighted at the arrival of his twin daughters. He named one of his daughters Nasira and the other Noltau. The old man brought up his daughters with a certain amount of difficulty. Whenever he went to fetch water or firewood he strapped one child on his stomach and the other on his back. He also carried the children while he was out grazing cattle, when he plastered the house, and while he did everything else. He endured many difficulties but nevertheless succeeded in bringing up his daughters until they were big girls.

When they were big enough to be left on their own, the old man locked up the girls in the house whenever he had to go out. They remained there until his return. When he came back, he would sing a song he had composed to alert his daughters, thus:

It had grown tender

But would not burst

My daughters of the knee

Nasira, Noltau, my beloved ones

Let me in.

On hearing the song, the children would immediately know it was their father and they would open the door for him.
This went on for a long time. Then, one day, some people from an enemy country came into the old man's village. They heard the voices of the two girls talking inside the house. They hid away in the nearby bushes to await the parents of the children whose voices they had heard. In the evening the old man returned and sang his usual song:

It had grown tender

But would not burst

My daughters of the knee

Nasira, Noltau, my beloved ones

Let me in.

The enemies listened to the old man's song. They spent the night in that country. Early next morning, the old man took his cattle out grazing, leaving the children locked up in the house. The enemies timed the old man, and on realising that he was about to return home they went to the door and sang his song, asking the girls to open the door for them. The girls did so thinking it was their father who had returned. Thereupon the enemies abducted the twin girls to their country.

The old man arrived soon after, but when he sang his usual song he received no response. Finding the door ajar, he entered, only to find no one in the house. He realised that his children had been stolen. He conducted a search for them far and wide, but to no avail. The old man had lost a wife and then his children because of his cruelty.

11 WHY PEOPLE HAVE TO DIG (LUHYA OF KENYA)

Long, long before our great-great-grandmothers were born, people never used to dig. They would take hoes to the garden, leave them there, and then go back in the evening to find that a portion of the shamba had been dug. They would take the hoes back to their homes and return them the next morning. There was in one of the villages of Bunyore a man who married a young bride. Usually, after a girl was married, she was expected to work very hard in order to be approved of as a good wife. So this woman whose name was Nyakowa woke up in the morning and started her daily duties. The work laid down for a young bride was quite a lot because she was expected to go to the river with a huge water pot which she had to lift on to her head all by herself. Next she had to grind a lot of millet within a very short time. These Nyakowa did with little difficulty, for she was renowned for industry long before she married her husband. With most of the work done, she next had to take the hoes to the shamba. As she walked towards the shamba, she pondered to herself, "If I went and started digging, wouldn't I dig a bigger area than the hoes do? And wouldn't I earn a lot of admiration in my new village?" Many questions like these flashed through her head, and she was full of excitement. By the time she reached the shamba she had already made up her mind what to do. So without hesitation Nyakowa took one of the hoes and started digging very vigorously. She expected praise from everybody who saw her. Little did she know that her rash action would end in disaster.

Indeed, she enjoyed the whole exercise from the beginning and was very proud of it. Although she thought her act a most heroic one, the ancestors were disappointed. They thought human beings were not being grateful because Nyakowa had failed to appreciate the kind offer from the god, Were Nyasaye.

And so the ancestors conspired with Were Nyasaye to have him end his merciful act to the people. They had been infuriated to learn that a young bride should go against this old custom which had prevailed long before they lived.

As time went on Nyakowa started to tire of the heavy work she was doing. The sun was moving west, so she decided it was high time she retired to the village. In any case, she told herself, hadn't she done more than the hoes did by themselves? She was sure she would be praised when people came to see the work she had done. However, in trying to please everyone, she pleased nobody. She explained what she had done, only to be met by reproach from everybody in her family and later in the whole village. Her bewilderment was such that she wished the earth could open up and swallow her. And what the people had feared proved true the next day. The hoes were taken to the shamba as usual, but they didn't dig. Those who had left them went in the evening to collect them, only to find them where they had left them.

People were therefore forced to take up their hoes and dig for themselves. And so, however strenuous it was, they were now forced to do it themselves. In the evening, people rushed to the young bride's home in anger. They were so enraged that they demanded she be sent back to her home. And so, the girl was ordered to go back to her people before anything serious was done to her. She immediately ran away. However, this did not change the situation. People had to continue digging since the normal custom had been violated. They had to wake up early every morning and go out to dig in the hot sun. They would only stop for lunch and then continue digging until evening.

So, when people think of their suffering their thoughts go back to the bride who dug, and they always blame her for her silly, ignorant act. That is why in Bunyore if a suitor wishes to marry a girl he will first go and spy on her, to see how much she can dig.

12 WHY ZEBRAS HAVE STRIPED SKINS (LUHYA)

Long ago before people started taking any other animal apart from the dog, it was said that donkeys could also be tamed. This rumour was told by one man who went to the bush to hunt. After killing the animal he had hunted he found that it was very heavy for him to carry alone. So he decided to find a way by which he could carry his prey. And as he was thinking, he saw a donkey pass nearby in the bush. All of a sudden an idea came into his head. He thought that if he took his prey and put it on the back of the donkey, it would help him carry his load. So he went after the donkey. He put the load on its back easily, for it did not attack him or run away.

He led the way until they reached his compound. After unloading the donkey he gave it food and it ate with appreciation. From this time on, this man kept the donkey.

This story went round that somebody had tamed a donkey. Soon the donkey was famous for its hard work throughout the village and the surrounding area. People wanted to satisfy their curiosity, and they soon set out to hunt for donkeys and use them to carry heavy loads. Donkeys did not know what was going on up to this time. They came to understand only after most of their friends had been taken away. They started to hide deep in the bushes. But all was in vain! People had realised that donkeys were very useful animals. So they made special efforts to hunt them down, wherever donkeys could be found. This problem really worried the donkeys. Many of their kind had been captured. The rumours they heard were horrifying. Rumour had it that those donkeys which had been captured were working too much and they were given only food enough to keep them going. This was indeed frightening. The rest of the donkeys decided to act quickly, lest they become victims of circumstance like their unfortunate friends. They therefore held an impromptu meeting. Here they discussed what should be done about the whole problem. One donkey suggested that they should seek help from Hare since he was known to be cunning and clever. All agreed that Hare should be asked for advice.

The next morning the donkey representative went to see Hare, who was only too willing to help. Hare asked him to tell all his friends to come to his compound early the next morning. This they did, and when they arrived they found Hare with whitewash in a huge can, ready to act. As the donkeys were not fast enough in thinking, they wondered how whitewash could have anything to do with their problem. Hare tried to explain but they seemed rather stubborn. Nobody was willing to be the first one to be experimented on. Finally, one donkey volunteered and stepped forward. Immediately, Hare set to work. He started painting stripes of whitewash on the donkey's skin. Soon the donkey had black-and-white stripes instead of being plain black or grey. As the first donkey was painted over, the other donkeys admired him. They all started wishing they could look like their friend. The moment that followed was full of struggle and scrambling over who should reach the paint first. The warning from Hare that they should be careful went unheeded. Hence, the struggling and fighting continued.It happened that after a number of donkeys had been painted, one donkey pushed to the front with such force that he stepped in the bucket that contained the whitewash. The whole bucket overturned pouring out all the paint. This was the end of everything. The remaining donkeys were helpless because they were the unfortunate ones. Hare told them that he could not help them any more because the fault had been theirs. And so, although the aggressive donkey was cursed for this bad act, nothing was done for their betterment, for the spilt paint could not be recovered. Hence, those donkeys that had been painted were safe from people's reach. They were the lucky ones and changed their name from donkeys to zebras. This name set them apart from the unfortunate donkeys who after this were all captured by men, and taken away to work for them. They were less fortunate and that is why they continue to be known as donkeys.

13 KALISANGA AND KALIYETO (LUHYA)

There was a man who married two wives. Both wives gave birth to a daughter each. The first wife called her daughter Kalisanga, whereas the second wife called hers, Kaliteyo. These step-sisters were born at almost the same time. They grew up together and were very fond of each other. Of these two, Kalisanga was the more beautiful. After a period of ten years Kalisanga's mother died, leaving her daughter under the care of her co-wife. As the girls matured they became even fonder of one another. When they went collecting firewood, they went together: when they went to fetch water from the stream, they were always together: when they went to bathe, they went together: when they ground grain, they did it together. In fact, they even shared a common boyfriend! But despite the great love the two sisters had for each other their mother hated Kalisanga and strove to find a way of destroying her. One day, with the intention of separating them, she assigned them different tasks to do at the same time. This she did so as to be able to carry out her plan for Kalisanga. Kaliteyo was asked to fetch water from the stream while Kalisanga was to remain at home and grind grain. As was their habit, the girls begged their mother to allow them to perform these two duties together, but she demanded that they do as she asked them to. Out of respect they obeyed her and did as she requested. When Kaliteyo took a water pot and left for the stream her mother called Kalisanga, who was grinding, into the house and stuffed her into a large drum. She then carried this away and threw it into a nearby lake. She then hurried back home and tried to appear calm as if nothing had happened.

When Kaliteyo returned from the stream and found her beloved sister missing, she asked her mother to tell her where Kalisanga had gone. The mother answered by saying she too had no idea. Immediately, Kaliteyo became uneasy and impatient. She went to her grandmother's place but did not find her sister. From there she went to each of her relatives but did not find Kalisanga. On her way home, she checked at their boy friend's home and she was told Kalisanga had not been there. Kaliteyo did not know what to think as she returned to her home. Once again she asked whether

Kalisanga had shown up while she was away, but was told they hadn't seen her yet, although their father too had looked for her everywhere. Kaliteyo felt very heart-broken and in distress, refused to eat any meals. She began to mourn the loss of her beloved sister who was her companion and with whom she worked.

One day she left home and went to the lake shore. She began to sing as follows:

Oh Kalisanga, Oh Kalisanga

My mother's child, Kalisanga

With whom will you grind?

With whom will you walk?

With whom will you collect firewood?

My mother's child, Kalisanga.

Kaliteyo sang that mournful song for some time. When she paused she heard a voice that sounded like that of a sick person, singing from the direction of the lake. She listened carefully and heard the voice sing:

Oh Kaliteyo, Oh Kaliteyo

My mother's child Kaliteyo

With your mother you will grind

With your mother you will walk, Kaliteyo

My mother's child Kaliteyo.

The song in answer to hers disturbed Kaliteyo very much. She repeated it again.

When she kept quiet again, she heard the voice answering her. Kaliteyo was convinced that the voice was her sister's and ran home to call her father. Their relatives and neighbours accompanied them to the lakeside. Again Kaliteyo began to sing as previously and Kalisanga too answered her as she had done earlier, with an even fainter voice which showed that she was nearing death as a result of hunger. Their boyfriend sang too and the drum in which Kalisanga was stuffed floated close to the shore and was removed from the water. It was opened up and Kalisanga was removed. One of her sides was virtually rotten. When Kaliteyo saw her sister so emaciated to the point of death she ran home and brought back sour milk together with porridge which she helped Kalisanga drink.

So the two girls refused to go back to their home but instead accompanied their boyfriend to his home and got married. Kaliteyo together with their husband carefully nursed Kalisanga until she healed. From then on they lived together in perfect love.

14 THE TORTOISE WHO FLEW
(A FOLKTALE FROM ZIMBABWE)

"Don't set sail using someone else's star," Tortoise's wife often cautioned him. This was her favorite proverb, and it was a good one to repeat to her husband, for he had his heart set on learning to fly. "I must visit my friend Osprey," Tortoise told his wife. "And how will I visit him if I do not learn to fly?"

Tortoise's wife shook her head. "Use your own star, dear husband. He is your friend. He'll understand."

But Tortoise fretted about this problem. He and Osprey were the best of friends, though nobody knows how their friendship began. Still, everyone could see that Osprey liked Tortoise. Many times, on his way home to the trees, Osprey stopped for a visit so that he could see his friend. Osprey had several times invited Tortoise to visit him in his treetop home, but Tortoise always found an excuse not to come, for he was reluctant to admit he had no way of getting up there to visit.

"Why not just explain that you cannot reach the treetops?" his wife asked. "He is your friend; he will understand."

"How can I let him down that way?" Tortoise asked. "I'll find a way." And so Tortoise went on thinking about how he might learn to fly. He watched the vultures and the storks, the egrets and the swallows, and he envied them with all of his heart. "If they can fly, why can't I?" he would cry. Hearing the cries, Hyena stopped by to laugh. "Have you learned to fly?" he cackled as he sauntered past. Warthog, Baboon, Cheetah, Waterbuck and Wildebeest laughed too. Everyone but Tortoise understood that he would never fly. Everyone did, that is, but Osprey, who eagerly awaited a visit from his friend. "Pity you can't climb trees," Monkey teased Tortoise. During the next few days, Tortoise wandered this way and that, searching his imagination and searching, too, every corner of the veldt. He was looking for some kind of wisdom, something that would help him learn to fly. And then one day as he squinted up at the big ball in the sky -- the sun, that is -- he suddenly knew just what to do. He hurried home. "I've got it!" he said to his wife. "I can fly, if only you will help me."

"But my dear," his wife said when he explained his plan, "no one should sail using someone else's star."

"But this is my dream!" Tortoise cried out, and because his wife loved him, she agreed to help.

The next morning, just as he had planned, Osprey appeared at Tortoise's home. He looked fit and handsome, for he had had a lovely morning soaring through the bright blue sky. "Is my friend Tortoise at home?" he called inside. But this morning Mrs. Tortoise answered. "I'm so sorry, but my husband had to go away," she said. "But he's left you a gift." And with that Mrs. Tortoise hauled out a big bundle of wrapped tobacco leaves; the bundle was neat and was tied up tightly with twine. "Why, thank you," Osprey said, and he picked up the bundle in his talons, spread his wings and flew toward his home. What Osprey did not know was that tied inside that bundle of tobacco was Tortoise. "Ahhh, how easy this was," Tortoise whispered to himself, and he could not help but smile as he thought how surprised his friend would be to see him when he opened the bundle of tobacco.

On they flew. The sun beamed down. Tortoise began to feel hot and sticky, and the leaves itched him. He hoped they would arrive very soon. Osprey simply flew on.

At last Tortoise came to the conclusion that he did not enjoy flying. "This is no fun at all," he thought.

Osprey continued to fly, and Tortoise began to feel more and more miserable. "Hey," he called at last, "let's land, can't we please …"

But before he could finish his plea, Osprey, startled by the sound coming from inside the bundle of leaves, opened his talons and let the bundle fall. Down, down, down the bundle tumbled toward the ground. "Help!" Tortoise cried, and all the animals within earshot heard this cry, but no one could see who was calling. When the bundle hit the ground, Tortoise burst free of the leaves. He was bruised and trembling with fright, but luckily the thick leaves had cushioned his fall.

Tortoise trundled home. "Oh my!" his wife cried when she saw the state of his shell. It was cracked in a dozen places. "What happened to you?" And when she heard the story, she couldn't help but laugh. "I told you never to sail using someone else's star. And never fly using another's wings," she added this time.

When Osprey heard the tale, he visited Tortoise to express his condolences. "We all have our place in this world, my friend," Osprey said, "and how marvelous your shell looks now."

And so it was Tortoise's gift, and warning, to all his descendants, for ever since that day, all tortoises have a pattern of cracks on their shells, the legacy of their ancestor's adventure.

15 THE LEGEND OF SHAKA ZULU (SOUTH AFRICA)

Once upon a time, there was a great African warrior named Shaka Zulu. He was the mightiest of valiant warriors in all the clans for miles around. Shaka could spear an animal in the bushes from up to 2 miles without making a single sound. His father was so proud of him, because of his skills on the battlefront. Shaka could lead an army of men into battle and not lose a single warrior. The name Shaka Zulu was feared by tribes from miles around and they had peace in his village for years.

Then one summer day, a Chief from another village approached Shaka with news that one of their rival clans was planning a secret attack on the village and he did not know when this was to take place. Shaka, knowing that he was still the most feared warrior for miles around, did not see this as a threat. He continued with his days as normal. The Chief from the other village approached Shaka one more time to warn him of the upcoming attack. This time Shaka spread the word to his fellow warriors, of the pending attack. The other men, did take this serious, and requested that Shaka speak with the village's Wise Council. Shaka felt differently though, because he was valiant, and a greater warrior, did not seek the advice of the wise council, and instead set out to hunt.

While away on the hunting trip, Shaka's village was attacked by the enemy. When he returned there was no one there, and not one hut was left standing. Feeling shocked and filled with grief Shaka retreated into the forest and was never seen or heard from again. In the meantime, his fellow villagers were treated with kindness and compassion from the enemy. They were intrigued by the knowledge that the Wise Council had to offer and welcomed them into the village rather then hold them as captives.
The moral of the story is to always seek Wisdom and Council rather your own personal, selfish desires. You never know whom you are putting at risk because of your careless decisions.

16 THE GRASSHOPPER AND THE TOAD

Grasshopper and Toad appeared to be good friends. People always saw them together. Yet they had never dined at each other's houses. One day Toad said to Grasshopper, "Dear friend, tomorrow come and dine at my house. My wife and I will prepare a special meal. We will eat it together." The next day Grasshopper arrived at Toad's house. Before sitting down to eat, Toad washed his forelegs, and invited Grasshopper to do the same. Grasshopper did so, and it made a loud noise.

"Friend Grasshopper, can't you leave your chirping behind. I cannot eat with such a noise," said Toad.

Grasshopper tried to eat without rubbing his forelegs together, but it was impossible. Each time he gave a chirp, Toad complained and asked him to be quiet. Grasshopper was angry and could not eat. Finally, he said to Toad: "I invite you to my house for dinner, tomorrow." The next day, Toad arrived at Grasshopper's home. As soon as the meal was ready, Grasshopper washed his forelegs, and invited Toad to do the same. Toad did so, and then hopped toward the food. "You had better go back and wash again," said Grasshopper. "All that hopping in the dirt has made your forelegs dirty again." Toad hopped back to the water jar, washed again, then hopped back to the table, and was ready to reach out for some food from one of the platters when Grasshopper stopped him: "Please don't put your dirty paws into the food. Go and wash them again."

Toad was furious. "You just don't want me to eat with you!" he cried. "You know very well that I must use my paws and forelegs in hopping about. I cannot help it if they get a bit dirty between the water jar and the table." Grasshopper responded, "You are the one who started it yesterday. You know I cannot rub my forelegs together without making a noise." From then on, they were no longer friends.

17 THE TORTOISE AND THE PRINCESS WHO NEVER SPEAKS

There was a king who had a daughter named Bola. Bola had never spoken a word and the king was very distressed. He had done all that he could to make Bola speak, powerful medicine men had brewed her all kinds of herbs and recited incantations but nothing worked. The king promised his daughter and half his kingdom to anybody who can make his daughter speak.

Tortoise heard of this reward and set out to get it. He bought a bottle of honey and placed it by a bush near where Bola lived while he hid himself. When Bola came by and saw the bottle of honey, she put her hand in it. Immediately Tortoise jumped out of his hiding place and grabbed Bola by the hand. Thief! He cried. So it is you! Who stole my honey and ate it!. I? Said Bola. Stole your honey to eat? Tortoise then tied Bola with a rope and started to lead her back to the palace singing,

Bola stole honey to eat

Kayin, Kayin

Bola is a cunning cheat

Kayin, Kayin

Bola is a shameless thief

Kayin, Kayin

To this, Bola sang in response,

Into the wood of the elephant I went with the elephant

Kayin, Kayin

Into the wood of the buffalo I went with the buffalo

Kayin, Kayin

And Tortoise has come to accuse me of stealing honey to eat

Kayin, Kayin

When they arrived at the palace, the king and all who were gathered were amazed to hear Bola sing. My daughter, who has never been heard to speak, speaks today! The king cried.

As he had promised he gave half his kingdom to Tortoise and Tortoise married the king's daughter.

18 THE THREE BROTHERS AND THE POT OF PORRIDGE

Three brothers were traveling through the dense rain forest jungle. They had been traveling on foot for almost a full day and night was falling. They needed a suitable place to rest for the night, a place where they would be safe from prowling animals of the night. They were in luck because before darkness fell, they spotted a little isolated hut in the distance. When they arrived at the hut, they met a kindly old woman who invited them in and offered them a place to spend the night. The old woman offered them some porridge which she was cooking in an iron pot over some firewood. The brothers declined for they were very exhausted and also did not want to impose on this old woman who living alone, had cooked enough porridge only for one person. The old woman gave them some mats and showed them into a room where they could lay down and have a good night's rest. Soon, the entire hut was dark and everyone in it was asleep.

Sometime in the night, the youngest of the three brothers woke up and he was very hungry. His older brothers had declined the offer of some supper and he had just gone along, but he was really hungry. So he went out into the kitchen to see if any of the porridge remained and indeed, there was enough porridge in there for one person. It appeared that the old woman had not eaten any of it, she must have been keeping it for the next day. It wouldn't harm anybody if he ate just a little bit of it, and it would certainly do him a lot of good. So he ate a little bit. Then a little bit more, and even more until it was all gone. Realizing his folly, he decided to cover it up and went out to pick some stones to put in the pot. He hoped the old woman would not notice.

The three brothers were up early the next morning to continue on their journey. They bade farewell to the old woman and thanked her for her kindness.

The old woman discovered the stones in her pot soon after the brothers left and immediately set out after them. Even though she was very old, she could move as fast, as or maybe even faster than any young man since she was able to catch up with the three young men. She accused them of stealing her porridge and filling her pot with stones, at which the eldest brother who spoke for them sincerely denied. The old woman though was certain that one of them performed the deed, so she challenged them to take a test. They went to a nearby river which had a log laying across it. Each one of them would walk across the river on the log while singing a song which the woman taught to them. They would each sing this song in Yoruba:

Ti m ba je koko arugbo

If I ate the old woman's porridge

Ki okun gbe mi, ki okun la mi

Let the sea take me

Ki okun gbe mi si erigidi ofun

Let the sea take me

The first two brothers walked confidently across the river singing the song. But the youngest brother was as scared as he walked and sang. His step faltered several times and he eventually fell into the river.

19 HOW THE CHIMPANZEES BOTTOM GOT SWOLLEN AND RED

Tortoise and Monkey were having a discussion when Monkey began to boast about how he would become king of all the animals saying 'Of all the animals, I am most like Man so I should be king' Monkey replied, 'You cannot be king for Lion is king and is very powerful' Tortoise replied, 'Yet, Man has power over Lion and I am most like Man'.

Tortoise felt threatened by this claim, not knowing what might happen if Monkey decided to start acting like Man. You see, Tortoise was not powerful, but what he lacked in strength, he made up in wit. And he knew and understood every animal's behavior so that he could outwit them all. But if the monkey was going to start acting in unpredictable ways, he did not want any of that. Tortoise decided to act quickly to put Monkey back in his place. Tortoise went home to prepare some akara (Bean cake) into which he added some fresh honey. When he was done, he put the akara in a basket and took it to Lion's house where he placed it just outside his door and left to hide behind a tree. The akara was warm and its aroma hung in the air so that Lion soon came out to see where it was coming from. He picked one ball of akara and ate it and this akara was sweeter than any akara he had ever eaten before. He ate another one, and then another one until all the akara was gone. Lion had a huge appetite and this was the best akara he had ever had, so he wanted some more. Who brought these akara? He bellowed but there was no answer. He searched the surrounding area and quickly found Tortoise. He grabbed Tortoise by the neck and asked him, how did these akara get here? Tortoise quivered and shook and frighteningly said I promised not to tell! But Lion insisted he tell or else?, so Tortoise confessed that it came from Monkey but it is a secret. He told Lion that, it was no akara at all but Monkeys feces which he keeps a secret.

Lion immediately headed to Monkeys house. When he saw Monkey, he asked him Give me sweet feces? Monkey was confused and gave Lion a blank stare. Lion roared at him 'I said give me sweet feces!' Monkey was terrified and defecated on the spot. It was not sweet and Lion was mad. He started to beat

Monkey while ordering him to make sweet feces until Monkeys bottom was all swollen and red.

Since then, Monkey has shelved his ambition to become king of all the animals.

20 THE LOST HEIR

A Very long time ago in a little village somewhere in the western part of the country now known as Nigeria, was a king who had three wives but no children. He needed a male heir to succeed him on the throne and he was worried. He decided to seek help from the ifa priest as he was growing old and time was short. The ifa priest came to the palace with his divinity board and cowries with which he consulted the oracle for a solution to the king's dilemma. The oracle revealed that the king would have one son but did not reveal which of the wives would bear the son. The oracle revealed that each would get pregnant after eating from a potion the priest would prepare. The ifa priest returned with a pot of stew into which he had mixed the potion for the three wives to share. The two older wives however were often wicked to the youngest wife, so they decided to keep the pot of stew for themselves. They believed that if the youngest wife did not eat from the stew, then they could be sure that she was not bearing the only son. When the youngest wife discovered the empty pot of stew, she started to cry for she had lost the opportunity to bear a child. In desperation, she scraped the pot with her fingers, licking every bit of leftover stew she could get.

Very soon, the two senior wives were spotting rounded bellies. And surprisingly, the third wife too started to exhibit a little bulge. All three wives were pregnant. Time passed and the two senior wives delivered their babies. They both had daughters. They now started to pay attention to the third wife, worried that she might have a son. When she was ready to give birth to her baby, the two senior wives were in attendance to help with the delivery. As soon as she gave birth, the baby boy was immediately taken away and replaced by a stone. The two senior wives quickly raised an alarm for they were shocked by what they had just delivered? A stone! The stone-mother soon became an outcast as the king sent her away from the palace and nobody in the village would have anything to do with her.

In the meantime, the baby boy had been wrapped in cotton cloth and taken into the forest where he was abandoned under a tree. A medicine man who lived deep in the forest and was out gathering herbs found him and took him home where he raised him into a fine gentleman. Many years passed and the king died, still without a male heir. The villagers needed to appoint another king but there was no obvious candidate, so the ifa priest was called. The oracle revealed that their king lived deep in the forest and would be found in the home of a powerful medicine man. A delegate was dispatched to go and fetch the would-be king.

The would-be kings Return to the village was welcomed by all but his origin was a mystery to everybody. The oracle had said that the boy's mother resides in the village but who could it be? Every woman in the village hoped that she was the mother no matter how unlikely it seemed. The mystery of king's mother needed to be solved before the coronation took place. The oracle advised that every woman should cook a pot of stew and bring it to the village square. The boy would taste from every pot, and from the taste he would identify his mother. Grand preparations began in every home. Every woman would cook the best pot of stew she had ever cooked in her whole life. A thousand and one ingredients and all manner of spices went into every pot, except for one pot, the one belonging to the village outcast. She lived in a little shack at the edge of the village and she had no money to buy ingredients for a pot of stew. She herself lived on fruits and vegetables that picked from her daily forages into the forest. When it was time for every woman to assemble in the market square, she placed what vegetables she could get into a pot with some water.

The aroma around the market square was overwhelming. There were miles of sizzling, delicious pots of stew. When the king-to-be arrived, everyone fell silent as he made his way from one pot to the other, tasting his way down the line. This went on for the whole day. Exhausted, he reached the last pot behind which sat an unkempt woman with ragged clothing. He tasted the content of her pot and burst into song, singing and proclaiming that this was his mother.

Thus, the wicked deed of many years past was uncovered and the two wicked wives were banished from the village.

21 WHY MOSQUITOES BUZZ IN PEOPLE'S EARS

A Very long time ago when Ear was a beautiful woman and ready for marriage, there were several suitors wooing her. There were big creatures, there were small creatures. There were fast and sleek creatures and there were slow ones. But they all professed their love for Ear and demonstrated their skills? And there was such an impressive array of skills that Ear had a difficult time making a decision. Then along came mosquito.   I would like you to be my wife, proposed Mosquito. Ear was so offended by this affront. Look around you! She cried. Of all the people and creatures in the whole world, what makes you think I can entertain such a thought? Ear was distressed. Marry you!! She continued you will be dead before the week is over. You're not strong, you're weak and I will never marry you!   Ear was exhausted from this tirade and she fell into her seat, fanning herself vigorously like she was trying to get any image of Mosquito out of her head. Meanwhile, Mosquito was really hurt by all that Ear said. It was very embarrassing to be talked to like that in front of all the other creatures who were whispering to each other and giggling. Apparently, they all agreed with Ear. Dead before the week is over Thought Mosquito as he slunk away. We'll see about that.

And from that day forward, whenever Mosquito sees Ear, he flies up to her and says Emi re, mi o ti ku, which in English means here I am, I am not dead!

But who did Mosquito eventually marry? And how did she get attached to either side of Head? That's another story I would like to hear.

ABOUT THE AUTHOR

A. Kwada was born and brought up in the northeastern part of Nigeria. He studied Computer science at the university and he loves writing, reading, and programming. He is also a blogger. He sees writing as a means of sharing the beauty of African Culture.

REFERENCE

Shaka Zulu"s pride. (n.d.). December 24, 2018, from http://myths.e2bn.org/mythsandlegends/userstory7608-shaka-zulus-pride.html

African folktales. (n.d.). Retrieved December 24, 2018, from https://www.worldoftales.com/African_folktales/African_Folktale_6.html

The Tortoise Who Flew (A Folktale from Zimbabwe). (2004). retrieved November 28, 2018, from https://www.uexpress.com/tell-me-a-story/2004/9/19/the-tortoise-who-flew-a-folktale

Folktales (n.d.) retrieved December 24, 2018 from http://www.allfolktales.com/folktales.php

Tyman, J. (n.d.). Kenyan Folktales retrieved November 27, 2018, from http://www.johntyman.com/africa/folk/

The legend of Moremi. (2015). retrieved November 27, 2018, from https://www.nairaland.com/2194936/legend-moremi

The story of Moremi. (2017). retrieved November 27, 2018, from http://omoyorubadfw.org/the-story-of-moremi/

Milton Keynes UK
Ingram Content Group UK Ltd.
UKHW012211061223
433851UK00008B/256